For Emma Cupitt

First published in Great Britain 1986
by Methuen Children's Books Ltd
11 New Fetter Lane, London EC4P 4EE
Copyright © 1986 Heather S. Buchanan
Printed in Great Britain

ISBN 0 416 53910 6

Matilda Mouse's Shell House

Heather S. Buchanan

Methuen Children's Books

It was a very hot day. Matilda stretched out on the mantelpiece behind a teapot where it was shady. She lived with her family inside the teapot, as it made a safe hiding place from the cat and the old lady who lived in the cottage. Sunshine streamed in through the kitchen windows, and bees buzzed about. It was nearly Midsummer Day.

Matilda worked hard in the teapot. There was always something to do, because her parents were often away, finding food for them all. Matilda had to keep her naughty twin brothers, Humphrey and Oliver, out of mischief and look after her little sister Rosie, helping her to get dressed and feed herself. Then the new baby, Holly, needed to be comforted when she cried, and rocked to sleep in her cradle.

Matilda *loved* having adventures. Before her brothers and sisters were born she used to go out of the teapot on her own to see what she could find in the cottage. She always felt excited when she thought about exploring, and although she loved her family, she longed to set off alone on another adventure.

She told her parents about her wish when they came home with some garibaldi biscuits for supper. They understood completely.

Her father tied some biscuit crumbs into
her headscarf. Her mother brought out a
little mother-of-pearl anchor and hung it
around Matilda's neck on a piece of silk,
to bring her luck. All the children hugged
her and felt almost as excited as she did.

When it was dark, all the mice climbed one after another out of the teapot and went with Matilda to the cottage door. They each hugged and kissed her again, and they all squeezed under the door to watch her scamper down the garden path. They waved and waved until they could no longer see her white headscarf in the moonlight.

The moonlight helped Matilda to see her way. She had not been walking for long when she reached the edge of the cliffs and saw the waves rolling on to the beach below her.

She climbed carefully down, and to her delight saw a sandcastle which the sea had not washed away. She decided to make it into a shell house.

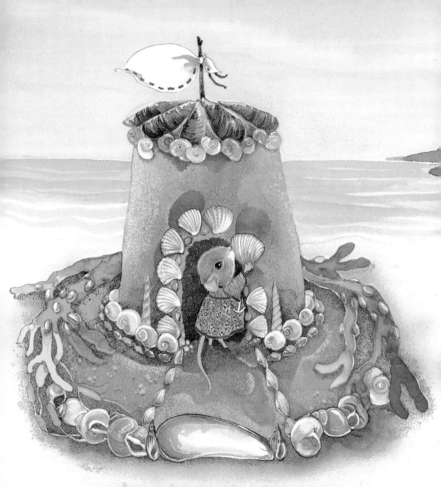

Matilda ate a few crumbs and curled up
beside the sandcastle. She was soon fast
asleep. The next morning she started
work and made a lovely space inside,
scooping out the sand with her front
paws. She fetched as many shells as she
could carry and carefully arranged them
to make a pattern on the roof and around
the door. Then she put seaweed all around
the sandcastle, to make a little garden.

Next she decided to make windows, so she burrowed two small holes in the wall, one either side of the door. It was lovely looking out of her little house and seeing the sea. She was just arranging some shells along the window-ledges when suddenly there was a terrible rushing noise and the whole sandcastle fell in on top of her. Matilda was terrified. She wriggled and pushed, but she could not get out.

Just when it seemed that all was lost, a little mouse in a stripey suit of red, white and blue came galloping across the beach to the rescue. He could see her toes sticking out of the sand. He grasped them and pulled hard. Out came Matilda, coughing and squeaking. He carried her to the sea where he gently bathed her face with water from a shell. When she opened her eyes he introduced himself. His name was George and he was on a seaside holiday with his family.

When Matilda felt better, George walked with her to a beautiful gipsy caravan which he had made out of wood all by himself. In it sat his five sisters, Bryony, Clover, Cowslip, Campanula and Daisy. They had painted the patterns on the caravan for him.

George's parents were there too. His mother soon had some camomile tea ready for Matilda to sip, and they wrapped her in a patchwork quilt because she was still shivering with shock.

Matilda stayed with George and his family for a few days, and they became great friends.

One day, George gently took Matilda's paw and asked her if she would marry him. She felt very happy, so she nodded. George explained that he would go back to decorate Tree Stump House with flowers, ready for their wedding, as is the custom of fieldmice, and then he would return for her. They were so happy that they danced all night on the beach.

When dawn came, George gave Matilda a beautiful pink shell, and she took the little anchor charm from around her neck and gave it to him as a keepsake. She waved and waved as the mouse family set off in the early morning light. When she could no longer see them, she scampered home as fast as she could to tell her family the wonderful news. She clasped the shell very tightly, and thought only of George all the way to the teapot.